BABUSHKA'S
MOTHER GOOSE

Patricia Polacco

PUFFIN BOOKS

With special thanks to my heroes,
Evgeny Rachev, Feodor Rojankovsky and Wanda Gág . . .
Much of the work in this book was inspired by their artwork.

PUFFIN BOOKS
Published by the Penguin Group
Penguin Putnam Books for Young Readers, 345 Hudson Street, New York, New York 10014, U.S.A.
Penguin Books Ltd, 27 Wrights Lane, London W8 5TZ, England
Penguin Books Australia Ltd, Ringwood, Victoria, Australia
Penguin Books Canada Ltd, 10 Alcorn Avenue, Toronto, Ontario, Canada M4V 3B2
Penguin Books (N.Z.) Ltd, 182-190 Wairau Road, Auckland 10, New Zealand

Penguin Books Ltd, Registered Offices: Harmondsworth, Middlesex, England

First published in the United States of America by Philomel Books, a division of The Putnam & Grosset Group, 1995
Published by Puffin Books, a member of Penguin Putnam Books for Young Readers, 2000

7 9 10 8 6

THE LIBRARY OF CONGRESS HAS CATALOGED THE PHILOMEL EDITION AS FOLLOWS:
Polacco, Patricia. Babushka's Mother Goose / Patricia Polacco. p. cm.
Summary: Presents a collection of traditional rhymes, rewritten to feature Russian characters and scenes.
1. Nursery rhymes, American. 2. Children's poetry, American. [1. Nursery rhymes. 2. American poetry.] I. Mother Goose. II. Title.
PZ8.3.P55895Bab 1995 398.8'0973—dc20 94-32332 CIP AC ISBN 0-399-22747-4

This edition ISBN 0-698-11860-X

Printed in the United States of America

*To Grammas, Bubbas, Nonas, Bushas, Babshkas, Bubbies and
Babushkas everywhere!*

Contents

Sources: "Day," "Yasha," "Three Babushkas," "Nina's Kittens," "The Little Angel," "Klootchka Plootchka," "Misha's Goat," "Matroishka," "Svetlana's Pancakes," "Billy Goat," "Birthday," "A Windy Day," "The Golden Child," and "Day Ending" are original nursery tales or rhymes by Patricia Polacco. "The Train to Ivanovo" is an original nursery tale by Patricia Polacco based on the nursery rhyme "The House That Jack Built." "Diadushka Planted a Turnip" and "The Clay Pot" are from Ukrainian folk tales retold by Carle Gaw, Patricia's babushka. "Babushka's Boot," "1, 2, Button My Shoe," and "A Little Pony" are tales from Mother Goose retold by Babushka Gaw. "The Crab, the Fish, and the Crane" and "Fox and Crane" are tales from Aesop retold by Babushka Gaw. "Stone Soup" is from a Moldavian folk tale retold by Babushka Gaw. "Diadushka's Nonsense Song" is an original verse by Patricia's grandfather George Gaw.

One of my earliest and most treasured memories was nestling into my Babushka's soft, ample lap. I snuggled in, full of expectation for a story, tale, or rhyme. As she began her telling, I would rest my ear on her breastbone and feel her voice resonate through to my soul. These precious moments are still the source of my well-being and trust of life itself.

My Babushka was, as all storytellers are, a great "borrower." She reshaped tales from Aesop, Mother Goose, and Moldavian folk tales, as well as other sources. She transformed them so that they reflected her own heart and homeland, the Ukraine.

And so, my dears, this book comes from my heart as a loving collection of some of her "retold" tales as well as my own, told in the same spirit. It is a tribute to my grandmother, my Babushka, and all grandmothers who hold little ones in their laps and fill their souls with wonder and joy.

—Patricia Polacco

Day

Sasha, Sasha, the sun is calling!
    It's peeking through your sill.
"Little one, I've brought the day,
    I'll race you up the hill.

"Get out of bed, dear little one,
    I've come a long, long way.
The cows are milked and chores are done—
    let's run and jump and play.

"Raise up your sleepy little head,
    I've brought a brand-new day.
Put on your clothes and make your bed—
    we'll do such things today!"

Yasha

Yasha had a beard
    that grew and grew and grew!

It reached down to the ground,
    it grew and grew and grew!

Up over fences, through a barn,
    and even past a hound,
It grew up goats, it grew down slopes,
    it grew without a sound.

It grew right here, it grew just there,
    it grew without a care.
It grew in, it grew out,
    it grew around a hare.

Yasha had the longest beard
that grew and grew and grew.
Now I wonder what you'll do
if it grows right up to you!

Three Babushkas

Three Babushkas lived in their bed.
One wore purple,
one wore red.
One wore ribbons and stripes and bows.
All of them lay there
and counted their toes.

Diadushka Planted a Turnip

Diadushka planted a turnip.
The turnip grew and grew until it was very very big.
Diadushka went to pick it.
He pulled and pulled,
　　　but he could not pull it out!

So he called Babushka.
Babushka pulled Diadushka,
and Diadushka pulled the turnip.
They pulled and pulled,
　　　but they could not pull it out!

So they called Anushka.
Anushka pulled Babushka,
Babushka pulled Diadushka,
Diadushka pulled the turnip.
They pulled and pulled,
　　　but they could not pull it out!

They called their dog, Katushka.
Katushka pulled Anushka,
Anushka pulled Babushka,
Babushka pulled Diadushka,
Diadushka pulled the turnip.
They pulled and pulled,
　　　but they could not pull it out!

They called their cat, Natasha.
Natasha pulled Katushka,
Katushka pulled Anushka,
Anushka pulled Babushka,
Babushka pulled Diadushka,
Diadushka pulled the turnip.
They pulled and pulled,
    but they could not pull it out!

Natasha called Ivana the mouse.
Ivana pulled Natasha,
Natasha pulled Katushka,
Katushka pulled Anushka,
Anushka pulled Babushka,
Babushka pulled Diadushka,
Diadushka pulled the turnip.
They pulled and pulled,
    but they could not pull it out!

Then along came a beetle, who bragged, "I'm big and stout!"

He pulled them all....

AND THEN THEY PULLED IT OUT!

Diadushka's Nonsense Song

Rum-a-suck-a
Pum-a-doodle.
Soup bag, pebble webble,
heem, hame, hime, ho…
Katooshka g-o-o-o-o!

Key-row
Ky-row
Kay-row…

Na-heem
Na-hime
Na-ho…

Rum-a-suck-a
Pum-a-doodle,
Soup bag, pebble webble,
heem, hame, hime, ho…
Katooshka g-o-o-o-o!

Nina's Kittens

Nina had five kittens,
   she cared not where they'd been.
But when she turned around,
   she saw that there were ten!

   She took in wash to keep them all—
      she really was so poor.
   But when she turned around again,
      there were a hundred more!

She dressed them up and put them out
 and kept them from the door.
But when she turned around again,
 there were a thousand more!

"What will I do!" she cried out loud.
 She couldn't see the floor.
But when she turned around again,
 there were a million more!

She loved them all and gave them names.
 Each one she did adore.
And when she turned around again,
 they loved her ever more!

The Clay Pot

There was a Fly who found a pot and took it for her home.
With winter coming, she kept it well
    but wished she weren't alone.

Then came a Gnat, who looked and sat.
    "Perfect for my home!"
Fly called out, "Come in, come in." Her voice was full of cheer.
    "The two of us can live so well.
You're very welcome here!"

Then came Frog, straight from a bog,
    "Perfect for my home!"

Fly and Gnat both called out, "Come in, come in," their voices full of cheer.
 "The three of us can live so well.
You're very welcome here!"

Then came Hare, without a care,
 "Perfect for my home!"
The three called out, "Come in, come in," their voices full of cheer.
 "The four of us can live so well.
You're very welcome here!"

Then up jumped Fox, with orange locks,
 "Perfect for my home!"
They all called out, "Come in, come in," their voices full of cheer.
 "The five of us can live so well.
You're very welcome here!"

Then Wolf came by, with a friendly sigh,
    "Perfect for my home!"
They all called out, "Come in, come in," their voices full of cheer.
    "The six of us can live so well.
You're very welcome here!"

At last came Bear, who cast his eye
    on that friend-filled pot.
"Can I come in?" he called with hope.
    They answered, "We think not!"
"But I'm alone, I need a home. Please, can I stay here?"

They thought awhile, then all called out,
    "Come in," they said with cheer.
"We *guess* we all can live quite well,
    Yes, you're welcome here!"

In went one paw, and then they saw
    the pot began to crack.
The friends all cried, "Take out your paw!"
    But Bear could not pull back.

It was too late. Oh, what cruel fate!
    The pot was cracked and broken.
The animal friends rolled on the ground,
    left cold and in the open.

"My dears," Bear said, "in truth I have a home
    in the forest there.
Please come with me," he sang with glee.
    "You've shown me that you care.

"Your hearts are dear,
    you should be here,
with me you'll now reside."
    And they were friends
from that day on,
    always by his side!

The Little Angel

There was a little angel,
　　who somehow lost her way.
She stopped and saw a little girl
　　and said, "Please come and play."

"I can't fly," sweet Kira said,
　　"but I hope you stay.
Come and jump upon my bed—
　　we'll laugh and bounce and play."

They jumped so high they touched the sky,
　　and then it was eleven.
The angel found that she was home,
　　but Kira was in heaven!

Klootchka Plootchka

Klootchka Plootchka,
    these are your toes.
Klootchka Plootchka,
    standing in a row.
Klootchka Plootchka,
    count your little toes.
Klootchka Plootchka,
    better hold your nose.

31

Misha's Goat

Misha had a goat,
    who ate his favored coat.
The goat spat out a button,
    that landed on a mutton.

The mutton took a leap,
    and jumped right on a sheep.

The sheep bumped a cow,
    who chased a big old sow.

The sow scared a duck,
    who made old Lowsha buck.

The horse chased a hen,
who flew up from her pen.

She landed on a hare,
who danced around a bear.

The bear ran through the yard,
uprooting all the chard.

"Me-oww," screamed the cat,
and on the goat she sat.

This was Misha's goat,
still eating Misha's coat.

Matroishka

There is Matroishka,
    who greeted Petroushka.
Then came Misha,
    who sang out to Greesha.
Out came Natasha,
    who danced with Sashuska,
and tiny little Anya,
    and even littler Vanya!
Now, who will put them all away
    so someone else can come to play?

Fox and Crane

Fox and Crane were friends. One day Fox invited Crane for dinner. Crane accepted the invitation, and Fox made some porridge and spread it out on plates.

Crane pecked and pecked at the plate with his long beak.

"Eat it up, Brother Crane," said Fox. "It's so very good—I made it myself."

Crane watched as Fox licked her place clean. Crane pecked and pecked, but could not get anything off the plate.

"Wasn't that a lovely dinner!" Fox exclaimed. "But you did not eat, my brother."

Crane sat silent, but then answered: "Sister Fox, I would be pleased if you could come to my house for dinner tomorrow night."

When Fox arrived, Crane had made a very delicious soup. He served the soup in tall jars with very narrow necks.

"Eat it up, Sister Fox. It's so very good—I made it myself."

Fox looked and looked at the jar. She turned it this way and turned it that way. She barked at it, she sniffed at it, but not a drop of soup could she get, for her head was too big to go into the long neck of the jar. She couldn't tip the jar, for she could not hold it with her paws.

But Crane put his long beak in the jar and relished every drop of his wonderful soup.

Fox was angry. Crane had given her tit for tat. But they valued their friendship, and from that time on, at each of their tables there was always a plate and always a jar.

38

Svetlana's Pancakes

Svetlana made some pancakes,
    big and flat and round.
She flipped them up,
    and they rolled out, bumping on the ground.

They rolled by trees, they caught the breeze,
    and sailed into the air.
They floated high and floated far,
    they flew without a care.

They flipped by trees and circled carts,
    they rolled by goats and jostled hens,
They rocked a cradle, gladdened hearts,
    and then came home again.

Billy Goat

Billy goat, billy goat, where have you been?
"Leaping the fence by the little red hen."

Where are the horses? Did they go astray?
"I saw Nikolka lead them away!"

Where are the geese? Did they fly away?
"Yes, they did, earlier today."

Where did they go? Off to see the Czar?
"Yes, they did—it's really not that far."

Where is Nikolka? Such a lazy lad.
"He's lying by the dacha—isn't he bad?"

Babushka's Boot

There once was a Babush
    who lived in a boot.
She had too many children,
    who cried with a hoot.
She gave them some borscht
    without any bread.
She kissed them all loudly,
    then sent them off to bed.

1, 2, Button My Shoe

1, 2

    button my shoe

3, 4

    there's the door

5, 6

    pick up sticks

7, 8

    must walk straight

9, 10

    fat little hen

11, 12

    dig and delve

13, 14

    Uri's courting

15, 16

    Tasha's stitching

17, 18

    there she's waiting

19, 20

    they'll have plenty

The Train to Ivanovo

This is the train to Ivanovo.

This is the bread
    under the bed
        on the train to Ivanovo.

This is the rat
    that ate the bread
    under the bed
        on the train to Ivanovo.

This is the cat
    that chased the rat
    that ate the bread
    under the bed
        on the train to Ivanovo.

This is the dog
    that worried the cat
    that chased the rat
    that ate the bread
    under the bed
        on the train to Ivanovo.

This is the goat
  with a crooked horn
  that tossed the dog
  that worried the cat
  that chased the rat
  that ate the bread
  under the bed
    on the train to Ivanovo.

This is the girl, tired and worn,
  that milked the goat with a crooked horn
  that tossed the dog
  that worried the cat
  that chased the rat
  that ate the bread
  under the bed
    on the train to Ivanovo.

This is the boy, shy and forlorn,
    that kissed the girl, tired and worn,
    that milked the goat with the crooked horn
    that tossed the dog
    that worried the cat
    that chased the rat
    that ate the bread
    under the bed
        on the train to Ivanovo.

This is the Babush, tattered and torn,
    who glared at the boy, shy and forlorn,
    that kissed the girl, tired and worn,
    that milked the goat with the crooked horn
    that tossed the dog
    that worried the cat
    that chased the rat
    that ate the bread
    under the bed
        on the train to Ivanovo.

Here is the hen that upset the corn
    that spilled on the Babush, tattered and torn,
    who glared at the boy, shy and forlorn,
    that kissed the girl, tired and worn,
    that milked the goat with the crooked horn
    that tossed the dog
    that worried the cat
    that chased the rat
    that ate the bread
    under the bed
        on the train to Ivanovo.

Here is the **farmer who** planted that morn
that fed **the** hen that upset the corn
that spilled on the Babush, tattered and torn,
who glared at the boy, shy and forlorn,
that kissed the girl, tired and worn,
that milked the goat with the crooked horn
that tossed the dog
that worried the cat
that chased the rat
that ate the bread
under the bed
on the train to Ivanovo.

Birthday

Pavel has a birthday,
    I think it is today.
Let's ask all the birds and fish
    to come and sing and play.

Masha has a birthday,
    I think it is today.
Let's ask all the kids to come—
    oh, I hope they stay!

A Little Pony

I had a little pony,
    it was a dapple gray.
It had a wavy mane
    that looked like curly hay.
I sold it to Babushka
    for her most prized brown goat.
And I'll not sing my song again
    without another coat.

A Windy Day

It was a very windy day—my kerchief blew away,
　　high into the sky it went, over by the bay.
A graceful crane flew by
　　and put it on her head.
Then she flew to see the Czar
　　and sat upon his bed.

A frog jumped past the sill that day
and landed on his nose.
"How dare you come and jump on me,
you know I am the Czar!"
With that he pulled Frog off his nose
and put it in a jar.

Out Frog jumped and bumped the crane
   and took the scarf away.
Then he hopped past Yasha's house
   and plopped into the bay.

A fish swam by and saw the scarf wrapped round the froggy head.
   "I'd love to have that pretty thing—it's perfect for my bed."
Mrs. Fox came to the pond and looked into the water.
   "I love your kerchief—may I have it? It's perfect for my daughter."

Young Fox wore it through the forest and ran into a bear.
"That scarf," Bear said, "may I wear it? I'll treat it with such care."

But it was a very windy day—the kerchief blew away.
    It blew high up into the air—

And landed on my hair!

The Crab, the Fish, and the Crane

Once there were three friends—
>a fish, a crab, and a crane.

"I need this stone," the crab called out one day to the others.
"Will you help me pull it to my home?"

"Of course we will," the other two replied.

So the crab tied each of them to the stone to help pull.

The three pulled and pulled and pulled.
They all pulled as hard as they could.

"Stop—there is something wrong," the crab called out.
"This stone is going nowhere!"

"I don't understand," the fish said. "I'm pulling as hard as I can."
"I don't understand either," the crane said. "I'm pulling as hard as I
>can too!"

"Well, I know that I'm pulling as hard as I can!" the crab announced.

The three of them sat for the longest time and stared at the rock.

After a time, the old badger that had been watching them came
>lumbering over.

"You are so silly!" he snapped.
"You are too close to see anything.
You are all eager to help, but only in your own way."

"The crane pulled *up* . . .
The fish pulled *into the water* . . .
The crab pulled *onto the shore* . . .
Of course the stone went nowhere!"

The three friends just looked at each other.

The Traveler

There was a lonely traveler,
    who walked the roads alone.
"Would you have some soup for me?
    Some bread? A leaf? A bone?"

"Soup for you!" the woman cried.
    "I have no soup for *me!*"
"Anything, I beg of you,"
    he said on bended knee.

From house to house he asked for food,
    but all were poor indeed.
"I've never seen such hungry souls—
    you all are in such need."

With that he set a pot to boil
    in the village square.
He picked up stones and tossed them in.
    Villagers began to stare.

"Such soup I'll make for you," he said.
    He stirred it with such glee.
One by one they came to watch
    to see what this could be.

"Soup from stones," a woman cried,
    "how can this really be?"
"Just bring me one of what you have,
    fetch it here to me!"

They each brought one and tossed it in,
    meager harvest from their toil.
Potatoes, onions, and sorgo gum—
    they stood and watched it boil.

Beets went in and chard did too—
    they pulled them from their carts.
The soup became a tasty stew.
    They watched and warmed their hearts.

"You're all invited, now feast with me!"
    the traveler said with glee.
"Come and sit and share this soup.
    Please come and eat with me!"

So many things he taught that day—
    mostly how to share.
But when they turned to thank the man,
    they saw he wasn't there.

The Golden Child

There is an ancient legend—
　　it's very old indeed—
about a child, a golden child,
　　who loves when there is need.

Enchanted child, with eyes so dear,
　　walks with God each day.
"Treat this one as you would me,"
　　the Lord came here to say.

But no one knows the golden child—
　　it looks like any other—
so every child it may be,
　　a sister or a brother.

Day Ending

The sun is down, sweet little one,
    the stars and moon have come.
Say sweet good night to all that sleep—
    your day is finally done.